AWKWARD

THE SOCIAL DOS AND DON'TS
OF BEING A YOUNG ADULT

KATIE SAINT, LPC, BCBA
— AND —
CARLOS TORRES, B.S.
═ ILLUSTRATED BY ═
MICHELLE LUND

AWKWARD : The Social Dos and Don'ts of Being a Young Adult

Authors - Carlos Torres and Katie Saint
Illustrator - Michelle Lund

First Edition First Printing

FUTURE HORIZONS INC.

721 W. Abram Street
Arlington, TX 76013
(800) 489-0727
(817) 277-0727
(817) 277-2270 (fax)
Email: info@fhautism.com
www.fhautism.com

Printed in the USA.

ISBN: 9781941765791

CONTENTS

FAMILY

NON–FAMILY RELATIONSHIPS

WORK

COMMUNITY

RESOURCES

FAMILY

DO PEOPLE FEEL LIKE I AM
A GOOD LISTENER?

DO

DON'T

- Do make eye contact with the person who is talking to you.

- Do nod your head to show that you are listening.

- Do make related comments and/or follow-up questions.

- Do offer suggestions if asked.

- Do recognize that sometimes people just want to vent.

- Do make validating statements.

- Do engage in conversation even if it is boring or something you don't care about.

- Don't give advice unless asked.

- Don't try to fix all of their problems.

- Don't change the subject too quickly.

- Don't walk away from the conversation before it's over.

- Don't interrupt the other person while he or she is talking.

- Don't multi-task while listening (such as using your phone or watching the TV).

- Don't try to "one up" the other person's story by telling a bigger or better story.

SCRIPT

Uncle Wally: *Hey, I just got a new stamp for my collection.*

You: *That's cool. What does it look like?*

Uncle Wally: *Well, it has a bird, a blue flower, some green grass, and clouds drifting in the background. It's the most beautiful stamp I've ever seen.*

You: *That's great. I am glad you like it so much.*

DISCUSSION QUESTIONS

1. What should you do if the topic is offensive to you?
2. What should you do if you are really bored and the person continues to talk for a long time?
3. What should you do if a person shares about self-harm or something equally serious?
4. Which topics are good to share with other family members?

SELF-ASSESSMENT

Directions: Answer the question and give yourself a score of 1, 2, or 3 based on the description below. Take the quiz multiple times during the next few months to see if you are improving.

Do people feel like I am a good listener?

1 = I struggle with this issue and it causes problems.

2 = I still need some help but issues rarely happen.

3 = I understand this issue and do it well.

DO I KNOW HOW TO ACCEPT GIFTS?

- Do say "thank you."

- Do come up with something positive to say about the gift no matter how you feel about it.

- Do get the person a gift for his or her birthday / special occasion if he or she did the same for you.

- Do re-gift a gift to a different friend group if you do not like the item.

- Do smile.

- Do recognize that someone gave you a gift to be affectionate.

- Don't accept a gift if it comes with a favor or expectation.

- Don't ask how much the gift cost.

- Don't say you don't like the gift.

- Don't feel obligated to show off the gift every time you see the person who gave it to you.

- Don't ask for the receipt.

- Don't brag about getting gifts.

SCRIPT

Friend: *Here you go. I got this for you.*

You: (You don't like or need the gift.) *Wow! A double sided ice-cream scooper! How cool!*

Friend: *Yeah! I got one for myself, too!*

You: *Awesome. So how about some ice cream?*

DISCUSSION QUESTIONS

1. What should you do if you don't like the gift?
2. What should you do if you already have the item?
3. What would you do if the gift was the wrong size?
4. How can you tell if someone enjoys the gift you gave to him or her?

SELF–ASSESSMENT

Directions: Answer the question and give yourself a score of 1, 2, or 3 based on the description below. Take the quiz multiple times during the next few months to see if you are improving.

Do I know how to accept gifts?

1 = I struggle with this issue and it causes problems.

2 = I still need some help but issues rarely happen.

3 = I understand this issue and do it well.

DO I KNOW HOW TO ADMIT I AM WRONG AND SAY SORRY?

DO

DON'T

- Do realize if you hurt someone's feelings.

- Do realize if you physically hurt someone by accident.

- Do apologize even if you didn't mean to be offensive.

- Do be mindful of your body language and tone of voice.

- Do pick the right place to apologize. (Don't do it in a big group of people unless you offended all of them.)

- Do ask the person how you can fix the problem.

- Don't say "sorry" if you don't mean it.

- Don't say "sorry" if you aren't going to change your behavior.

- Don't use an "I'm sorry but ____" statement.

- Don't apologize to people for every little thing.

- Don't use an apology to make people feel bad for you.

SCRIPT

You: *Wow, your hair is really short!*

Friend: *Ugh. That's offensive! My barber messed up.*

You: *Sorry. I didn't mean to offend you. It was just a big change I was not ready for. I do think it looks good, though.*

DISCUSSION QUESTIONS

1. What might happen if you say "sorry" but don't mean it?
2. What should you do if you apologize but your friend doesn't accept your apology?
3. How can you tell if saying "sorry" isn't enough?
4. When is it okay to not say "sorry?"
5. What should you do if it is unclear why someone is mad at you or why you should apologize?

SELF-ASSESSMENT

Directions: Answer the question and give yourself a score of 1, 2, or 3 based on the description below. Take the quiz multiple times during the next few months to see if you are improving.

Do I know how to admit I am wrong and say sorry?

1 = I struggle with this issue and it causes problems.

2 = I still need some help but issues rarely happen.

3 = I understand this issue and do it well.

DO I KNOW HOW TO RESPOND TO SOMEONE TALKING ABOUT SOMETHING I DON'T LIKE?

- Do listen and ask follow-up questions to show understanding.

- Do make eye contact and nod your head to reassure the other person that you're listening.

- Do contribute to the conversation if you have any helpful comments.

- Do remember that if you listen well to others, they will listen better to you.

- Do understand that caring about a friend's interests is a characteristic of being a good friend.

- Don't change the subject.

- Don't look bored.

- Don't check your phone.

- Don't make unrelated comments.

- Don't give short, one-word responses.

SCRIPT

Friend: *So, today I went and played tennis with my dad and he was beating me by two. I came back and was able to get close. I was only one point away.*

You: (Nod head.) *Nice!*

Friend: *I then hit the ball so hard it zoomed right by him and I scored another point to tie it up!*

You: *Good work! I'm not the best tennis player.*

DISCUSSION QUESTIONS

1. What should you do if the person keeps talking about the subject?
2. What should you do if you don't know what to comment or say back to the person?
3. What should you do if the person never listens to your stories?
4. How can you tell if someone is bored with your stories?

SELF–ASSESSMENT

Directions: Answer the question and give yourself a score of 1, 2, or 3 based on the description below. Take the quiz multiple times during the next few months to see if you are improving.

Do I know how to respond to someone talking about something I don't like?

1 = I struggle with this issue and it causes problems.

2 = I still need some help but issues rarely happen.

3 = I understand this issue and do it well.

DO I KNOW HOW AND WHEN TO SAY NO TO FAMILY?

- Do say "no" less often to your family than to your friends.

- Do realize it is okay to say "no" if it makes you uncomfortable.

- Do realize it is okay to say "no" if it could hurt you or someone else.

- Do realize it is okay to say "no" if you are morally against the question or activity.

- Do say "no" if you're not capable of doing what the person is asking of you.

- Do say "no" if it would put your job or relationships at risk.

- Do be honest about why you are saying "no."

- Do make sure to explain the reason that you're saying "no" so the other person does not feel bad.

- Don't let someone take advantage of you.

- Don't be afraid to try new things.

- Don't let your anxiety stop you from saying "yes."

- Don't lie when talking about your accomplishments or completed tasks. Especially, don't lie about meaningless information (such as if you saw a movie or not).

- Don't lie or make up excuses for why you are saying "no."

- Don't let your emotions control your answer.

SCRIPT

Mom: *Hey, can you come over and help paint our living room today?*

You: *No, I'm sorry I can't because my wrestling tournament is today. I can come over tomorrow.*

Mom: *Sure, tomorrow would be great. Thanks so much! Good luck at your tournament!*

DISCUSSION QUESTIONS

1. What should you do if a family member is pressuring you to say "yes?"
2. What topics are okay to say "no" to?
3. How can you tell if someone is taking advantage of you?
4. What should you do if your family member is mad at you for saying no?

SELF-ASSESSMENT

Directions: Answer the question and give yourself a score of 1, 2, or 3 based on the description below. Take the quiz multiple times during the next few months to see if you are improving.

Do I know how and when to say no to family?

1 = I struggle with this issue and it causes problems.

2 = I still need some help but issues rarely happen.

3 = I understand this issue and do it well.

DO I KNOW HOW TO ACT AND TALK WHEN I AM AROUND FAMILY?

DO

DON'T

- Do talk about what you have done since the last time you saw your family members.

- Do ask about how your family members are doing.

- Do be kind and patient with kids.

- Do be a good listener when people are talking about themselves.

- Do try to chat with every person at least a little bit.

- Do show respect, especially to elders.

- Do help with kids and senior citizens in the family.

- Do help clean up.

- Don't swear unless it's commonly done by all of the family members present.

- Don't talk about controversial topics.

- Don't start arguments with your family.

- Don't brag.

- Don't bring up any family issues.

- Don't bring up any distasteful topics.

- Don't always be the first one to start eating.

SCRIPT

Uncle: *Ezra scored a touchdown last week at his game!*

You: *Nice. What position does he play?*

Uncle: *He is the starting running back for the team.*

You: *That is awesome. I have always wanted to play wide receiver.*

DISCUSSION QUESTIONS

1. What would you do if a family member brought up an uncomfortable topic?
2. What would you do if you had nothing to add to the conversation or didn't know what to talk about?
3. How should you address a family member if you don't get along?

SELF-ASSESSMENT

Directions: Answer the question and give yourself a score of 1, 2, or 3 based on the description below. Take the quiz multiple times during the next few months to see if you are improving.

Do I know how to act and talk around family?

1 = I struggle with this issue and it causes problems.

2 = I still need some help but issues rarely happen.

3 = I understand this issue and do it well.

DO I KNOW WHAT TO DO WHEN OTHER PEOPLE FIGHT OR ARGUE?

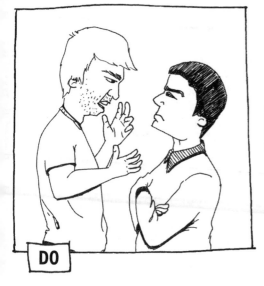

DO

DON'T

- Do keep your opinions to yourself.

- Do give them space.

- Do find something else to do.

- Do remain neutral.

- Do act normally when the fight is over.

- Do try to remove yourself from the situation.

- Don't make eye contact with the people having the argument.

- Don't make comments or get involved.

- Don't try to change someone's opinion.

- Don't pick a side.

SCRIPT

Uncle Teddy: *Luke "The Crusher" is the best wrestler of all time!*
Aunt Sally: *No way. Chuck Towers is hands down the best.*
Uncle Teddy: *You are such a blockhead! You don't know anything!*
Aunt Sally: *You are a nincompoop!*
You: (Walk away and don't make eye contact.)

DISCUSSION QUESTIONS

1. What should you do if the argument turns physical?
2. What should you do if they don't stop fighting?
3. What should you do if they bring you into the argument?
4. How can you redirect others around the situation?

SELF-ASSESSMENT

Directions: Answer the question and give yourself a score of 1, 2, or 3 based on the description below. Take the quiz multiple times during the next few months to see if you are improving.

Do I know what to do when other people fight or argue?

1 = I struggle with this issue and it causes problems.

2 = I still need some help but issues rarely happen.

3 = I understand this issue and do it well.

DO I KNOW HOW TO PLAN A FAMILY EVENT?

DO

DON'T

- Do make sure to contact all members of your extended family that you want to invite.

- Do organize what each person will bring to the get-together.

- Do be flexible about what people will bring.

- Do allow others to help plan the event.

- Do have adult and kid-friendly activities planned if kids will attend.

- Do offer snacks and beverages.

- Don't be upset if things don't go 100 percent your way.

- Don't leave anyone in the family out (even people who live out of town).

- Don't be controlling about the event.

- Don't talk down to family members or make them feel unwelcome.

- Don't bring up uncomfortable conversations.

SCRIPT

Grandma: *Hi, honey. What should I bring to the party tonight?*

You: *Can you bring your famous bread?*

Grandma: *Sure, I'd love to whip up a batch.*

You: *Great! Thanks, Granny!*

DISCUSSION QUESTIONS

1. What would you do if you didn't want to invite all of your family members?
2. What should you do if your family members have different opinions about how to run the event?
3. What should you do if conflict arises at the event?
4. What should you do if things don't go according to your plan?

SELF-ASSESSMENT

Directions: Answer the question and give yourself a score of 1, 2, or 3 based on the description below. Take the quiz multiple times during the next few months to see if you are improving.

Do I know how to plan a family event?

1 = I struggle with this issue and it causes problems.

2 = I still need some help but issues rarely happen.

3 = I understand this issue and do it well.

NON-FAMILY RELATIONSHIPS

DO PEOPLE THINK MY HOUSE LOOKS ACCEPTABLE?

DO

DON'T

- Do mow your grass approximately once per week.

- Do shovel within twenty-four hours of a snowfall.

- Do keep your yard clear of clutter.

- Do your dishes when or before the sink is full.

- Do put your laundry away.

- Do have dirty laundry discreetly put in hamper (usually in bedroom).

- Do vacuum and/or sweep and mop.

- Do organize any belongings in spaces guests will use.

- Do put away hygiene or personal items.

- Do make sure the bathroom is clean (sink, toilet, mirror, shower/tub, and floor).

- Don't put offensive pictures where the neighbors can see them.

- Don't put off small maintenance repairs.

- Don't leave messes.

- Don't let things get moldy.

- Don't keep your clothes in the washer or dryer for more than two hours.

- Don't leave the stove on.

SCRIPT

Guest: *Hey, your house looks really nice.*

You: *Thanks! I cleaned the house all morning!*

Guest: *The yard looks really nice, too.*

You: *Thanks. I got to use my new lawn mower.*

DISCUSSION QUESTIONS

1. What would people think if you had pictures of girls or guys in their swimsuits on your wall?
2. What would your girlfriend or boyfriend think if your house was a mess?
3. What would your neighbors think if your yard was not shoveled or mowed?
4. If there was an emergency, what would happen if your house was too cluttered to get out or for rescue workers to get in and help you?

SELF—ASSESSMENT

Directions: Answer the question and give yourself a score of 1, 2, or 3 based on the description below. Take the quiz multiple times during the next few months to see if you are improving.

Do people think my house looks acceptable?

1 = I struggle with this issue and it causes problems.

2 = I still need some help but issues rarely happen.

3 = I understand this issue and do it well.

DO I GET ALONG WITH MY ROOMMATE?

DO

DON'T

- Do discuss rules and personal boundaries.

- Do keep your things clean.

- Do clean up shared spaces after use.

- Do discuss solutions with your roommate in a calm voice when problems arise.

- Do be quiet if your roommate is sleeping.

- Do be friendly and occasionally ask your roommate to hang out.

- Do recognize when your roommate is busy and needs to be left alone.

- Do be respectful when your roommate has friends over.

- Do pay rent and shared bills on time.

- Don't overtake shared space.

- Don't be loud during sleep hours (different per roommate).

- Don't assume you are invited to your roommate's activities.

- Don't look through your roommate's personal belongings.

- Don't eat your roommate's food or drink his or her beverages.

- Don't talk on the phone in the same room that your roommate is in.

- Don't be naked in front of your roommate.

- Don't use your roommate's personal belongings.

- Don't get behind on rent or shared bills.

SCRIPT

You: *Hey, how was work today?*

Roommate: *Good. How was your day?*

You: *Pretty good, but I didn't have a bowl to eat my cereal out of this morning.*

Roommate: *Oh, I know. I have been so busy that I haven't had time to do the dishes.*

You: *Do you want to do them together so it takes less time?*

Roommate: *Sure, that would be great. Thanks.*

DISCUSSION QUESTIONS

1. What would you do if your roommate did not respond well when they were confronted about a problem?
2. What would you do if your roommate went through your stuff?
3. What would you do if you and your roommate did not agree on a TV show to watch together?
4. What would you do if your roommate had a boyfriend or girlfriend over?

SELF-ASSESSMENT

Directions: Answer the question and give yourself a score of 1, 2, or 3 based on the description below. Take the quiz multiple times during the next few months to see if you are improving.

Do I get along with my roommate?

1 = I struggle with this issue and it causes problems.

2 = I still need some help but issues rarely happen.

3 = I understand this issue and do it well.

DO PEOPLE THINK I AM A GOOD HOST?

DO

- Do make sure your house smells nice and looks clean.

- Do offer something to drink and/or eat. Prepare this ahead of time.

- Do show first-time guests where the bathroom is located.

- Do have a few ideas of activities that most of your guests would like.

- Do make sure your house is not too hot or too cold.

- Do make sure any controversial items are put away.

- Do plan well and invite people over with enough time for them.

- Do wear clothes that match the event. (*Example: sweatshirt and jeans are fine for a movie, but not for dinner.*)

- Do introduce people if they do not know each other.

DON'T

- Don't bring up controversial or offensive conversations.

- Don't invite someone you aren't comfortable with.

- Don't invite more people than your house/activity can handle.

- Don't provide snacks that the guests are unlikely to enjoy.

- Don't single anyone out in an activity or conversation.

- Don't leave or ignore your guests.

- Don't let your guests get out of control (which could result in trouble from your landlord, neighbors, or police).

- Don't be selfish or rude.

- Don't let your guests wait outside too long after they ring the doorbell or knock.

SCRIPT

You: *Thanks for coming over!*

Friend: *Thanks, it will be fun. I brought chips.*

You: *Great, come on in. Would you like a grape soda?*

Friend: *Sure.*

You: *Great, take a seat. We are watching the game. Let me introduce you to my friends.*

DISCUSSION QUESTIONS

1. What are some examples of activities that would require a short notice or a long notice?
2. What would you do if one of your guests did not want to do one of the activities you planned?
3. What should you do if one of your friends gets out of control?
4. What should you do if people are not respecting your property?
5. How would your guests feel if you only paid attention to one of them?
6. What could be a solution if you didn't have food and drinks to offer to your guests?

SELF–ASSESSMENT

Directions: Answer the question and give yourself a score of 1, 2, or 3 based on the description below. Take the quiz multiple times during the next few months to see if you are improving.

Do people think I am a good host?

1 = I struggle with this issue and it causes problems.

2 = I still need some help but issues rarely happen.

3 = I understand this issue and do it well.

DO PEOPLE THINK I AM A GOOD GUEST?

DO

DON'T

- Do bring a snack or drink.
- Do say "thank you."
- Do respect friends' house rules.
- Do clean up after yourself.
- Do introduce yourself to people you don't know.
- Do be flexible with the activities.
- Do bring up small talk.
- Do look presentable based on the activity.
- Do be friendly with all guests.
- Do let your host know in advance that you are coming.
- Do knock or ring the doorbell. Wait for your friend to answer.
- Do ask others about themselves.

- Don't go into anyone's personal room unless invited.
- Don't bring up controversial or offensive topics.
- Don't say negative things about people.
- Don't complain about the activities.
- Don't be the center of attention.
- Don't wear anything that would make you stand out.
- Don't help yourself to food or drinks which were not offered.
- Don't demand group activities.
- Don't refuse to participate.
- Don't forget to let your host know if you are not coming.
- Don't just walk into their home.

SCRIPT

Friend: *Hi. Thanks for coming over.*
You: *Thanks for having me. I brought soda.*
Friend: *Great, thanks. Come on in. This is Ted.*
You: *Hi, Ted. Nice to meet you. I'm Slick Vic.*
Ted: *Hi, nice to meet you! Did you catch the game last night?*

DISCUSSION QUESTIONS

1. What should you do if the food is not good?
2. What would people think if you didn't talk very much?
3. What would people think if you came dressed in your pajamas?
4. What would people think if you dominated the conversation?

SELF-ASSESSMENT

Directions: Answer the question and give yourself a score of 1, 2, or 3 based on the description below. Take the quiz multiple times during the next few months to see if you are improving.

Do people think I am a good guest?

1 = I struggle with this issue and it causes problems.

2 = I still need some help but issues rarely happen.

3 = I understand this issue and do it well.

DO I LOOK PRESENTABLE?

DO

DON'T

- Do take a shower at least every other day or immediately after any physical activity.

- Do put on deodorant daily.

- Do brush your teeth at least twice a day.

- Do make sure your clothes are clean.

- Do make sure your clothes are appropriate for the occasion. (See Appropriate Attire Examples in the Resource section of this book.)

- Do comb your hair every day.

- Do trim and clean fingernails.

- Do shave armpit and leg hair (women).

- Do keep hair groomed and cut per your style or preference (including facial hair).

- Don't smell bad.

- Don't have any stains or holes in clothing unless it was made that way.

- Don't put on too much cologne or perfume.

- Don't forget to brush your teeth.

- Don't forget to comb your hair.

- Don't forget to use deodorant.

- Don't have patchy facial hair.

- Don't wear offensive t-shirts (which includes subject matters like swearing, sexual content, or death).

- Don't let your hair get tangled.

SCRIPT

Friend: *Wow! You look really nice today.*

You: *Thanks, I just got my hair cut. Check out my new shoes!*

Friend: *Awesome, what kind of cologne do you use?*

You: *Thanks. It's "Smells Good" by Carlito. So, what are our plans for tonight?*

Friend: *I think we are getting together at The Crusher's house.*

DISCUSSION QUESTIONS

1. What would you do if you didn't dress the same as your friends or peers?
2. What would happen if you smelled bad?
3. What would happen if you had bad breath?
4. What would happen if you went to work in clothes that are too casual?

SELF-ASSESSMENT

Directions: Answer the question and give yourself a score of 1, 2, or 3 based on the description below. Take the quiz multiple times during the next few months to see if you are improving.

Do I look presentable?

1 = I struggle with this issue and it causes problems.

2 = I still need some help but issues rarely happen.

3 = I understand this issue and do it well.

DO I INTERACT WELL IN GROUPS?

DO

DON'T

- Do talk about topics that interest the group.

- Do try to relate to everyone.

- Do show you are listening by maintaining eye contact.

- Do confirm you agree by nodding your head and/or using affirming statements (such as "yes," "uh huh," and "I agree").

- Do introduce yourself to group members you don't know.

- Do maintain good hygiene.

- Do talk about what others are talking about. (Some topics are more appropriate in social groups than at work.)

- Do use jokes to relate to friends and pay attention to their responses to make sure your jokes are appropriate for the group.

- Don't belittle or talk down to someone.

- Don't insult the group's interests.

- Don't interrupt other group members while they are talking.

- Don't invite people to the group without asking others in the group first.

- Don't talk behind any member's back.

- Don't dominate the conversation.

- Don't use your phone during group discussions.

- Don't leave the group prematurely.

SCRIPT

Friend: *Hey, Slick Vic. Who is coming to volleyball tonight?*

You: *I think The Crusher, Teddy, and Pint-size Jess.*

Friend: *Great. Do you plan on sticking around for some dinner after our game?*

You: *Oh yeah! Victory chicken wings sound great!*

DISCUSSION QUESTIONS

1. What conversation topics are more appropriate for social situations compared to work?

2. How do you know if your conversation is appropriate or offensive?

3. What would you do if you didn't want to do what the group is doing?

SELF–ASSESSMENT

Directions: Answer the question and give yourself a score of 1, 2, or 3 based on the description below. Take the quiz multiple times during the next few months to see if you are improving.

Do I interact well in groups?

1 = I struggle with this issue and it causes problems.

2 = I still need some help but issues rarely happen.

3 = I understand this issue and do it well.

DO I REALIZE WHEN MY FRIENDS ARE BORED?

DO

DON'T

- Do read facial expressions (if they have not changed after fifteen minutes).

- Do change the topic or activity if you recognize that your friend is bored.

- Do find activities that all people are interested in.

- Do ask other people what they would like to do.

- Do give others the chance to talk.

- Do ask others questions about themselves.

- Do show others that you are interested in them or their hobbies.

- Don't ask if your friend is bored.

- Don't ignore your friends or leave them out.

- Don't take total control of the situation.

- Don't talk for more than two minutes at a time.

- Don't get up and leave.

- Don't do something unexpected just to get a reaction from your friends.

SCRIPT

Friend: (Looks bored and yawns.)

You: *So … what should we do today?*

Friend: *Let's go work out or play some basketball.*

You: *That sounds way better than sitting here doing nothing.*

DISCUSSION QUESTIONS

1. What should you do if you are bored?
2. What would you do if you did not want to do the activity that your friends were doing?
3. What should you do if you can't find something to do that interests your friends?
4. At what point is it okay to go home or end hanging out?
5. What would you do if you had a great story but your friends weren't listening?

SELF–ASSESSMENT

Directions: Answer the question and give yourself a score of 1, 2, or 3 based on the description below. Take the quiz multiple times during the next few months to see if you are improving.

Do I realize when my friends are bored?

1 = I struggle with this issue and it causes problems.

2 = I still need some help but issues rarely happen.

3 = I understand this issue and do it well.

DO I KNOW HOW TO GET OUT
OF UNCOMFORTABLE SITUATIONS?

- Do try to change the topic.

- Do cover up any nervous body language or facial expressions.

- Do switch to a new activity.

- Do use jokes or humor to distract the other person from the uncomfortable topic.

- Do let the person know if the majority of the conversations make you feel uncomfortable.

- Do ignore the comment if it was just said in passing.

- Do stay in the conversation if it is important to your friend.

- Don't say that you are uncomfortable.

- Don't giggle or make awkward body movements.

- Don't continue in the conversation if you feel uncomfortable.

- Don't add to the conversation to make the other person think that you are interested.

- Don't be mean when you respond to the person.

SCRIPT

Friend: *Hey Vic, who are you going to vote for?*

You: *Dude, did you see that sweet car that just drove by? I want to go test drive one!*

Friend: *Oh, cool! Yeah, I would want a blue one, though.*

DISCUSSION QUESTIONS

1. What would you do if the person kept talking about the subject?
2. What would you do if the person was your boss or authority figure?
3. Who can you talk to if the conversation makes you feel unsafe?
4. How can you tell if you make someone feel uncomfortable?

SELF-ASSESSMENT

Directions: Answer the question and give yourself a score of 1, 2, or 3 based on the description below. Take the quiz multiple times during the next few months to see if you are improving.

Do I know how to get out of uncomfortable conversations?

1 = I struggle with this issue and it causes problems.

2 = I still need some help but issues rarely happen.

3 = I understand this issue and do it well.

DO I KNOW WHEN I BRAG
OR TALK ABOUT MYSELF TOO MUCH?

- Do read facial expressions and body language of the people you are talking to.

- Do let others talk in the conversation.

- Do ask questions about others to take the attention off yourself.

- Do recognize that it's okay to feel good about your accomplishments and skills.

- Do be aware that your body language and facial expressions can help or hurt the conversation.

- Don't always talk about your accomplishments or skills every time you talk to a person.

- Don't constantly talk about yourself.

- Don't act like you're better than people.

- Don't reply to a friend's comment by saying that you did something better.

SCRIPT

You: *Hey, I beat level seven of Lava Man.*

Friend: *That's cool. Was it hard?*

You: *It was pretty hard, but I beat it. How was your soccer game last night?*

DISCUSSION QUESTIONS

1. How do you know if you offend someone by talking about yourself too much?
2. What would you do if your friend talked about himself or herself all the time?
3. How can you tell if someone thinks you are bragging?
4. When is it okay to talk positively about yourself?

SELF-ASSESSMENT

Directions: Answer the question and give yourself a score of 1, 2, or 3 based on the description below. Take the quiz multiple times during the next few months to see if you are improving.

Do I know when I brag or talk about myself too much?

1 = I struggle with this issue and it causes problems.

2 = I still need some help but issues rarely happen.

3 = I understand this issue and do it well.

DO I GIVE PEOPLE ENOUGH SPACE?

DO

DON'T

- Do read facial expressions or body language to tell if a person is annoyed or content with the space you are giving him or her.

- Do back off if the person seems annoyed or uncomfortable.

- Do realize that every person has different needs for space.

- Do give extra space if you are unsure of the person's boundaries.

- Do recognize that different settings require different space.

- Do be casual about giving yourself space if someone invades your area.

- Don't invade a person's space.

- Don't ask a person if he or she needs more space.

- Don't be so far away that you make people feel uncomfortable.

- Don't make a big deal out of apologizing for invading someone's space. Just say sorry and change your behavior.

SCRIPT

You: (Get in line to wait for a movie.)

Random Person: (Turns around and gives you an annoyed look.)

You: *Oh, I am sorry.* (Back up a few steps.)

DISCUSSION QUESTIONS

1. How can you tell if you are in someone's personal space?
2. What should you do if someone is in your space?
3. How much space is too much space?
4. What are examples of scenarios in which more or less space would be needed?

SELF–ASSESSMENT

Directions: Answer the question and give yourself a score of 1, 2, or 3 based on the description below. Take the quiz multiple times during the next few months to see if you are improving.

Do I give people enough space?

1 = I struggle with this issue and it causes problems.

2 = I still need some help but issues rarely happen.

3 = I understand this issue and do it well.

DO I KNOW HOW TO DEAL WITH SECRETS?

- Do determine if the secret is a fun secret or a hurtful secret.

- Do realize that this person has trust in you and that is why they told you the secret.

- Do realize that you can break someone's trust if you tell a secret.

- Do tell your secrets (not someone else's) to people you trust.

- Do get to know a person before sharing secrets with them.

- Do realize that not every person is trustworthy.

- Don't keep secrets about suicide or situations that can cause harm.

- Don't tell people, "I know _____'s secret."

- Don't bother or interrupt someone in order to tell them a secret.

- Don't tell someone a secret that you don't want people to know.

- Don't tell secrets to people you just met or don't know.

- Don't tell people that you have a secret if you aren't going to tell them what it is.

SCRIPT

Friend: *Dude, I have to tell you something! I just got my first kiss! You can't tell anyone yet.*

You: *Congrats man. Don't worry, I won't tell anyone.*

Friend: *Great! I knew I could trust you and just had to tell my best friend.*

DISCUSSION QUESTIONS

1. What should you do if someone says he or she will hurt you if you tell anyone and the secret is something that needs to be told to authorities?
2. What should you do if your friend is suicidal?
3. What would you do if a friend told people your secret?
4. Who are good and bad examples of people to tell secrets to?
5. What should you do if you are unsure if a secret could be hurtful?

SELF-ASSESSMENT

Directions: Answer the question and give yourself a score of 1, 2, or 3 based on the description below. Take the quiz multiple times during the next few months to see if you are improving.

Do I know how to deal with secrets?

1 = I struggle with this issue and it causes problems.

2 = I still need some help but issues rarely happen.

3 = I understand this issue and do it well.

DO I KNOW HOW TO RESPOND
TO A FRIEND WHO IS SAD?

DO

GET OVER IT.

DON'T

- Do listen and ask follow-up questions to show understanding.

- Do make eye contact and nod your head to reassure your friend that you're listening.

- Do contribute to the conversation if you have any helpful comments.

- Do remember that if you listen well to others, others will listen better to you.

- Do understand that caring about a friend's interests is a characteristic of being a good friend.

- Do recognize that some friends may want you to just listen.

- Do realize that it is okay if you cannot fix their problem.

- Do recognize that some people might want a hug and others won't.

- Don't change the subject.

- Don't look bored.

- Don't check your phone.

- Don't make unrelated comments.

- Don't give short, one-word responses.

- Don't offer solutions unless your friend asks for ideas.

- Don't try to solve your friend's problem for him or her.

SCRIPT

Friend: *Slick Vic, my grandma died this morning and I have no one else to talk to.*

You: *I'm sorry. I have never met her but I'm sure she was an awesome lady. What was one of your favorite things to do with her?*

Friend: *We used to eat hard candies and watch old reruns of our favorite shows.*

You: (Nod head.) *Cool!*

DISCUSSION QUESTIONS

1. What should you do if the person is crying?
2. What should you do if your friend is suicidal?
3. What would you do if you were the reason they were sad?
4. How can you tell if someone is really feeling better after the conversation?
5. What should you do if you have a friend who constantly comes to you with problems?

SELF-ASSESSMENT

Directions: Answer the question and give yourself a score of 1, 2, or 3 based on the description below. Take the quiz multiple times during the next few months to see if you are improving.

Do I know how to respond to a friend who is sad?

1 = I struggle with this issue and it causes problems.

2 = I still need some help but issues rarely happen.

3 = I understand this issue and do it well.

DO I KNOW HOW AND WHEN TO SAY NO?

DO

DON'T

- Do say "no" if someone wants you to do something that is not safe or will get you in trouble.

- Do offer something else if you are going to say "no."

- Do consider if you will benefit from the request.

- Do recognize that if you continue to say "no" to many things, friends will stop asking you. (This can be good or bad.)

- Do push yourself out of your comfort zone.

- Do give a concrete answer in order to stay away from words like "maybe," "possibly," etc.

- Don't let friends take advantage of you.

- Don't be afraid to try something new.

- Don't let others talk you into doing something you don't want to do.

- Don't get upset if the majority of your friends say "yes," but you say "no."

- Don't say "no" too many times.

- Don't say "yes" if you actually mean "no."

SCRIPT

Friend: *Hey, do you want to go explore that abandoned building?*

You: *No, thanks. I don't want to get caught by the cops. Let's go get lunch instead.*

Friend: *Come on! Don't be a wimp.*

You: *No, man! I don't want to pay a ticket if we get in trouble. I would rather play video games at my house.*

DISCUSSION QUESTIONS

1. What should you do if your friends try to pressure you to say "yes?"
2. What would you do if saying "no" could cause you to lose a friend?
3. How can you tell if your choice would be a safe one?
4. How can you tell if you are saying "no" too often or not enough?

SELF-ASSESSMENT

Directions: Answer the question and give yourself a score of 1, 2, or 3 based on the description below. Take the quiz multiple times during the next few months to see if you are improving.

Do I know how and when to say no?

1 = I struggle with this issue and it causes problems.

2 = I still need some help but issues rarely happen.

3 = I understand this issue and do it well.

DO I KNOW HOW AND WHEN TO TEXT A FRIEND?

DO

DON'T

- Do skip the small talk.

- Do be brief.

- Do send pictures if they are relevant to the conversation.

- Do respond as soon as possible.

- Do realize that sarcasm and joking are hard to read over text.

- Do use a symbol to communicate jokes or sarcasm e.g., "lol," "haha," or ":)."

- Do realize that short, one-word answers can be interpreted that you are uninterested.

- Do take turns initiating the conversation.

- Don't message people much more than they message you.

- Don't send more than three messages in a row before the other person responds.

- Don't send messages that could be viewed as harassment.

- Don't send inappropriate or unwanted pictures.

- Don't ask people to send you inappropriate pictures.

- Don't hassle people if they don't respond.

- Don't send extremely long messages via text.

- Don't talk about serious issues over text message.

SCRIPT

You: *Hey, did you see the game?*
Friend: *Yeah! It was amazing.*
You: *I can't believe Brad Brizzle made that three-pointer at the last second!*
Friend: *Yeah, and that pass from Wayne Diesel was phenomenal.*
You: *We should really try to get to a game before the playoffs are over.*
Friend: *For sure. Let's invite the crew.*

DISCUSSION QUESTIONS

1. What are some examples of times you should call instead of text?
2. How do you know when someone is not interested in texting?
3. What are some examples of things you can text to friends but not to family or co-workers?
4. What should you do if you are not interested in the conversation?

SELF-ASSESSMENT

Directions: Answer the question and give yourself a score of 1, 2, or 3 based on the description below. Take the quiz multiple times during the next few months to see if you are improving.

Do I know how and when to text a friend?

1 = I struggle with this issue and it causes problems.
2 = I still need some help but issues rarely happen.
3 = I understand this issue and do it well

DO I KNOW HOW TO TALK TO A FRIEND ON THE PHONE?

DO

DON'T

- Do be aware of your location and surroundings.

- Do have a greeting when answering the phone or calling a friend.

- Do realize that your tone of voice affects the conversation. (See Tone of Voice Exercises in the Resource section of this book.)

- Do realize and respect if your friends have different opinions than you.

- Do make statements so they know you are listening.

- Do have a concluding statement to end the conversation.

- Do try to have a back-and-forth conversation.

- Don't drag the conversation on if you have nothing to talk about.

- Don't rush the conversation if the other person has a lot to talk about.

- Don't have long silent pauses.

- Don't talk too loudly or quietly.

- Don't mumble.

- Don't just give one-word answers.

- Don't eat while talking on the phone.

- Don't call people if you have nothing important to talk about.

- Don't do private things while talking on the phone.

- Don't call if you can get your message across in a short text.

SCRIPT

You: *Hey, how are you today?*
Kathleen: *Great. How are you?*
You: *Good. So, what are our plans for tonight?*
Kathleen: *I thought the plan was to meet up with everyone at the game?*
You: *That's right. Anyway, could you give me a ride?*
Kathleen: *Sure. I'll pick you up at six.*
You: *Sounds good. See you then.*
Kathleen: *Later.*

DISCUSSION QUESTIONS

1. What would you do if you wanted to end the call but your friend didn't?
2. What should you do if you are uncomfortable with the conversation?
3. What should you do if you cannot reach someone after calling twice?
4. What would you do if someone called you too much?
5. How often is too much to call someone?
6. When is it too late or too early to call someone?

SELF-ASSESSMENT

Directions: Answer the question and give yourself a score of 1, 2, or 3 based on the description below. Take the quiz multiple times during the next few months to see if you are improving.

Do I know how to talk to a friend on the phone?

1 = I struggle with this issue and it causes problems.
2 = I still need some help but issues rarely happen.
3 = I understand this issue and do it well.

DO I KNOW HOW TO USE SOCIAL MEDIA APPROPRIATELY?

DO

- Do post things that interest you and your friends.

- Do realize there is a difference between publicly posting and private messaging people.

- Do think about who will see your post.

- Do use social media to keep up with friends and things of interest.

- Do be careful not to bother your friends with too many requests or messages (see Texting page).

- Do use social media to organize groups or events.

- Do block people if they are annoying you or harassing you.

- Do only post pictures of people who want their pictures posted on social media.

DON'T

- Don't post controversial topics or pictures (such as money, religion, sex, politics, etc.).

- Don't vent about your problems.

- Don't trust everything you see or read on social media.

- Don't accept friend requests from, or send them to, people you have never met face-to-face.

- Don't confront someone publicly on social media.

- Don't post hurtful things on social media.

- Don't start unnecessary debates or arguments on social media.

- Don't meet up with people who you only met through social media.

- Don't post something that could get you in trouble at work.

SCRIPT

You: (Thinking to yourself.) *I wonder if it would offend anyone if I posted an article about the Boston Buffalo.*

I know most of my friends are Milwaukee Sidewinder fans, but I am allowed to have my own opinions on sports.

This shouldn't hurt anyone's feelings since it's about sports and is not a controversial topic.

DISCUSSION QUESTIONS

1. What would you do if someone posted something that offends you?
2. What should you do if you accidentally post something inappropriate?
3. How do you know if you are posting too much or bothering someone?
4. What should you do if someone blocks you?

SELF-ASSESSMENT

Directions: Answer the question and give yourself a score of 1, 2, or 3 based on the description below. Take the quiz multiple times during the next few months to see if you are improving.

Do I know how to use social media appropriately?

1 = I struggle with this issue and it causes problems.

2 = I still need some help but issues rarely happen.

3 = I understand this issue and do it well.

DO I INTERACT WELL WITH FRIENDS AT RESTAURANTS?

DO

DON'T

- Do talk about topics that interest the group.

- Do use your napkin to wipe your face.

- Do have good hygiene.

- Do be aware if people are giving you weird looks; it may mean that you are doing something outside of the social norm.

- Do order clockwise unless the group decides to do it differently.

- Do assume that you will be paying for your own meal.

- Do thank others if they pay for your meal.

- Do look for an opportunity to buy some else's meal if they bought yours previously.

- Don't talk with your mouth full.

- Don't talk loudly because other people are also trying to have conversations.

- Don't swear or talk about topics that are not appropriate for kids if children are present.

- Don't eat until everyone has their food.

- Don't talk about gross bodily functions or gory topics.

- Don't dominate the conversation.

- Don't take up too much space at the table.

- Don't reach across the table.

- Don't eat off other people's plates.

SCRIPT

You: *Hey, Pint-size Jess, what are you going to order?*

Friend: *I don't like anything here. Who picked this place?*

You: *I picked it. It's a new restaurant and I wanted to check it out. How about you pick next time?*

Friend: *Okay, I guess I can just order a burger.*

You: *I will pay this time since you got the check last time.*

DISCUSSION QUESTIONS

1. What is an example of a conversation you can have about accepting someone paying for your meal?
2. How should you handle it if you don't like anything at the restaurant?
3. What are some conversations that you should avoid?

SELF-ASSESSMENT

Directions: Answer the question and give yourself a score of 1, 2, or 3 based on the description below. Take the quiz multiple times during the next few months to see if you are improving.

Do I interact well with friends at restaurants?

1 = I struggle with this issue and it causes problems.

2 = I still need some help but issues rarely happen.

3 = I understand this issue and do it well.

DO I KNOW HOW TO GET A BOYFRIEND OR A GIRLFRIEND?

- Do treat the other person in the same way that you want to be treated.

- Do pursue someone who has common interests.

- Do establish a friendship first.

- Do pick someone of equal attractiveness.

- Do pursue someone with similar morals and values.

- Do respect the other person's body and boundaries as well as your own.

- Do be confident.

- Do try to look your best.

- Do give compliments.

- Don't try to get intimate too fast.

- Don't send more messages than the other person sends.

- Don't change your personality in order to get the other person to like you.

- Don't be afraid of rejection.

- Don't make excuses as to why the other person won't like you.

- Don't try too hard by doing something you wouldn't normally do or by being insincere.

- Don't ignore the other person's interests.

SCRIPT

You: *Wow, you look really nice tonight.*

Potential boyfriend or girlfriend: *Thanks, I bought this outfit just for tonight.*

You: *I am really glad you did. We could see this movie with our favorite actor in it.*

Potential boyfriend or girlfriend: *Yeah, I am so excited! I have seen all of his movies.*

DISCUSSION QUESTIONS

1. How can you tell if the other person likes you?
2. What should you do if you are not sure how they feel?
3. What should you do if they don't like you?
4. What are some factors that would make you not want to date a person?

SELF-ASSESSMENT

Directions: Answer the question and give yourself a score of 1, 2, or 3 based on the description below. Take the quiz multiple times during the next few months to see if you are improving.

Do I know how to get a boyfriend or a girlfriend?

1 = I struggle with this issue and it causes problems.

2 = I still need some help but issues rarely happen.

3 = I understand this issue and do it well.

DO I KNOW HOW TO MAINTAIN A RELATIONSHIP?

DO

- Do treat the other person in the same way that you want to be treated.

- Do resolve conflict in a calm manner.

- Do make time to have fun together.

- Do let little things go.

- Do compromise.

- Do be a good listener.

- Do respect the other person's family.

- Do be affectionate regularly.

DON'T

- Don't call the other person names.

- Don't be messy.

- Don't cheat on the other person with someone else.

- Don't be verbally or physically abusive.

- Don't be controlling.

- Don't forget anniversaries or important dates.

- Don't talk down to the other person.

SCRIPT

You: *Hey, how has work been going?*

Your significant other: *My boss isn't listening to my ideas and I am getting frustrated.*

You: *That stinks. You have really great ideas. What are you going to do about it?*

Your significant other: *I don't know, but you are always a great listener. It always makes me feel better. Thank you.*

DISCUSSION QUESTIONS

1. What would you do if your significant other was doing something that you didn't like?
2. How do you know if your partner is happy in the relationship?
3. What things could make your significant other unhappy?

SELF-ASSESSMENT

Directions: Answer the question and give yourself a score of 1, 2, or 3 based on the description below. Take the quiz multiple times during the next few months to see if you are improving.

Do I know how to maintain a relationship?

1 = I struggle with this issue and it causes problems.

2 = I still need some help but issues rarely happen.

3 = I understand this issue and do it well.

WORK

DO PEOPLE AT WORK RESPECT ME?

- Do initiate appropriate work conversations.

- Do complete your work.

- Do have some small talk with minor personal details.

- Do show empathy toward others at work and make reassuring statements.

- Do be friendly with your boss.

- Do understand that it is okay if some people don't like you.

- Do work hard.

- Do be a team player.

- Do ask people casual questions about themselves.

- Do participate in activities outside of work with co-workers (for example, a Christmas party).

- Don't ever raise your voice at co-workers.

- Don't be lazy.

- Don't blame others.

- Don't report co-workers for minor issues.

- Don't over-correct people.

- Don't purposely exclude yourself.

- Don't ask too many questions.

- Don't act like an expert.

- Don't dominate conversations.

- Don't complain or be too negative.

SCRIPT

Co-worker: *Hey, Slick Vic, nice job on that last project.. You nailed it.*

You: *Thanks. It was a real group effort.*

Co-worker: *Yeah, we should all go out to dinner tonight to celebrate.*

You: *Awesome, I will send an email to the rest of the crew.*

DISCUSSION QUESTIONS

1. What would you do if you felt like you were not respected at work, and how would you change it?
2. What are the characteristics of co-workers whom you do or do not respect?
3. What could you do that would hurt your reputation?
4. How could you show respect to your co-workers?
5. How could you show respect to your boss without being a suck-up?

SELF-ASSESSMENT

Directions: Answer the question and give yourself a score of 1, 2, or 3 based on the description below. Take the quiz multiple times during the next few months to see if you are improving.

Do people at work respect me?

1 = I struggle with this issue and it causes problems.

2 = I still need some help but issues rarely happen.

3 = I understand this issue and do it well.

DO I CHAT WELL WITH MY CO-WORKERS?

- Do initiate small talk.

- Do ask co-workers about their weekend or any weekend plans.

- Do make eye contact.

- Do keep personal space.

- Do be friendly to co-workers you may not like.

- Do use your break time to catch up with your co-workers.

- Do keep your work relationships as friendships rather than as romantic or sexual ones.

- Do chat about weather, sports, or other current events.

- Don't speak badly of others.

- Don't bring up controversial or offensive topics.

- Don't overshare about your personal life.

- Don't be rude to others when they initiate conversation.

- Don't complain about your job.

- Don't talk instead of work.

- Don't interrupt others while they're talking.

- Don't swear.

- Don't share about inappropriate or sexual things you may do in your personal time.

SCRIPT

Co-worker: *Hey man, we have a lot of work today. How was your weekend?*
You: *Great! I watched the game. How was your weekend?*
Co-worker: *It was fun. I hung out with my friends.*
You: *Sounds fun! Want to help me move these boxes?*

DISCUSSION QUESTIONS

1. What should you do if someone makes a comment that makes you feel uncomfortable?
2. What would your co-workers think if you talked more than you worked?
3. What would your co-workers think if you didn't talk to them?
4. What should you do if you are tired or having a bad day?
5. What is inappropriate to talk about at work?

SELF-ASSESSMENT

Directions: Answer the question and give yourself a score of 1, 2, or 3 based on the description below. Take the quiz multiple times during the next few months to see if you are improving.

Do I chat well with my co-workers?

1 = I struggle with this issue and it causes problems.
2 = I still need some help but issues rarely happen.
3 = I understand this issue and do it well.

DO I SPEAK WITH MY BOSS WELL?

- Do keep small talk to a minimum.

- Do address job-related topics.

- Do make eye contact.

- Do keep personal space.

- Do be friendly to your boss.

- Do share a personal issue if it impacts your job and performance.

- Do recognize that it is your boss' job to hold you accountable.

- Do ask for help if you do not know how to do something.

- Don't say negative things about others.

- Don't interrupt your boss while he or she is talking.

- Don't over-share about your personal life.

- Don't be rude to others when they initiate conversation.

- Don't complain about your job unless you are looking for a reasonable solution.

- Don't share about inappropriate or sexual things that you may do in your personal time.

- Don't swear when talking to your boss.

- Don't become defensive while you receive feedback.

SCRIPT

You: *Good morning, Craig. I was wondering if you heard anything about the change in my schedule.*

Boss: *Yes, Slick Vic. Thanks for giving me enough time to see that you needed time off for a family vacation. I will give you the paperwork by the end of the day.*

You: *Thanks, Craig! I'll bring you back a keychain.*

Boss: *Sounds good! Hey, Slick Vic, keep up the good work!*

DISCUSSION QUESTIONS

1. What should you do if your boss is upset with you?
2. How do you know what issues are important enough to ask questions about or tell to your boss?
3. How do you know when to tell your boss about co-worker issues?
4. What should you do if you know that your boss is having a bad day?
5. How do you know what is appropriate to talk about with your boss?

SELF-ASSESSMENT

Directions: Answer the question and give yourself a score of 1, 2, or 3 based on the description below. Take the quiz multiple times during the next few months to see if you are improving.

Do I speak with my boss well?

1 = I struggle with this issue and it causes problems.
2 = I still need some help but issues rarely happen.
3 = I understand this issue and do it well.

DO I KNOW WHEN PEOPLE NEED SPACE AT WORK?

- Do read facial cues and body language.

- Do back off if your co-worker is giving you short answers.

- Do back off if your co-worker says that he or she is having a bad day.

- Do give space and leave the other person alone if you can tell that he or she is concentrating.

- Do give space if you can tell that others are having a conversation.

- Do realize that space may be needed when people are not upset.

- Do remember to respect that you and others have work to complete.

- Don't continue to ask questions if the other person is unresponsive.

- Don't complain if people need space.

- Don't take it personally if a co-worker talks to some people but not you.

- Don't interrupt a conversation.

- Don't ramble on without giving someone else a chance to respond.

- Don't make eye contact or stare at a person while giving him or her space.

- Don't argue about people needing space or hassle them about it.

SCRIPT

You: *Hey man, do you have a minute?*

Co-worker: *Hang on. I am in the middle of something.*

You: *Okay, I will be at my desk.* (Think to self, *He seems pretty busy. I will let him come to me when he is free.*)

Co-worker: (Five minutes later.) *Hey, sorry. I just needed time and space to finish up that project. Thanks for waiting.*

DISCUSSION QUESTIONS

1. What are some facial cues and body language signs that could tell you that someone needs space?
2. What should you do if you have a time-sensitive question?
3. What should you do if someone isn't giving you space?
4. What should you do if you need to work together with someone to complete your project?

SELF-ASSESSMENT

Directions: Answer the question and give yourself a score of 1, 2, or 3 based on the description below. Take the quiz multiple times during the next few months to see if you are improving.

Do I know when people need space at work?

1 = I struggle with this issue and it causes problems.

2 = I still need some help but issues rarely happen.

3 = I understand this issue and do it well.

DO I RESOLVE MY OWN CONFLICT AT WORK?

DO

DON'T

- Do compromise with co-workers to find a solution.

- Do determine if the issue is big enough to address. (If you are unsure, ask a trusted person outside of work.)

- Do take time to calm your emotions first, and keep a calm tone of voice.

- Do read facial expressions when interpreting how the other person is viewing the conflict.

- Do ignore issues that are not worthy of confrontation.

- Do involve your manager or boss if you are not able to resolve the conflict yourself.

- Do make sure the compromise is fair for both sides.

- Do make eye contact, stand / sit up straight, and talk with confidence.

- Don't use "always" or "never" statements.

- Don't try to resolve the conflict over email or text message.

- Don't instantly blow up or get defensive if you are confronted with a conflict.

- Don't talk down to people when resolving a conflict.

- Don't raise your voice or swear.

- Don't call people names.

- Don't show nervousness.

- Don't bring others into the conflict unless they share the same issue.

SCRIPT

You: *Hey, do you have a minute? I want to talk with you about work.*

Co-worker: *Yeah, sure, I am not doing anything. I have all day!*

You: *I've finished my project and I have been assigned to help you with yours. I can do Section A. Can you do Section B by Friday?*

Co-worker: *Eh, Friday might not work. I don't know if I will be in.*

You: *I think it is fair if we divide the project. If you feel you cannot complete your part, maybe we should see what the manager thinks.*

DISCUSSION QUESTIONS

1. What is an example of a big or small issue?
2. What would you do if you could not reach a compromise or agreement?
3. When should you involve a boss?
4. What would you do if your co-worker made false promises?

SELF-ASSESSMENT

Directions: Answer the question and give yourself a score of 1, 2, or 3 based on the description below. Take the quiz multiple times during the next few months to see if you are improving.

Do I resolve my own conflict at work?

1 = I struggle with this issue and it causes problems.

2 = I still need some help but issues rarely happen.

3 = I understand this issue and do it well.

DO I UNDERSTAND SARCASM AT WORK?

- Do understand that not everything people say is always true, and they might be joking.

- Do realize that sarcasm may seem rude, but it is not intended to be that way.

- Do understand that you should not use sarcasm all the time (especially with your boss or customers).

- Do read facial expressions when interpreting sarcasm.

- Do be careful when using sarcasm because it can easily be misinterpreted as something hurtful.

- Do use sarcasm to say something funny about yourself rather than about others.

- Don't use sarcasm in serious situations.

- Don't use sarcasm to hurt others.

- Don't use sarcasm in arguments.

- Don't use sarcasm when communicating through electronic messaging.

SCRIPT

You: *I've accomplished so much today that I am going to give myself a raise!*
Co-worker: *Yeah, while you're at it, you might as well give us all a pay raise.*
You: *If only I could do that... right?*
Other Co-worker: *Well, back to work. Break is just about over for me.*

DISCUSSION QUESTIONS

1. What are some examples of sarcasm?
2. What should you do if someone is using sarcasm in a hurtful way?
3. How could sarcasm get you into trouble?
4. When should you not use sarcasm?

SELF-ASSESSMENT

Directions: Answer the question and give yourself a score of 1, 2, or 3 based on the description below. Take the quiz multiple times during the next few months to see if you are improving.

Do I understand sarcasm at work?

1 = I struggle with this issue and it causes problems.
2 = I still need some help but issues rarely happen.
3 = I understand this issue and do it well.

DO I MANAGE MY EMOTIONS WELL WHEN STARTING A NEW JOB?

- Do learn as much as you can about the job in advance.

- Do something to calm yourself before entering the workplace.

- Do talk with a trusted friend about anything you are nervous about.

- Do be positive.

- Do give your best effort even when it is hard.

- Do socialize with others.

- Do make work friends so you can ask them questions.

- Do talk to your boss.

- Do remember that your job will get easier with experience.

- Do remember that the harder you work, the faster and easier your job will become.

- Don't engage in self-defeating or negative thoughts (such as telling yourself, "I will suck at this").

- Don't avoid the job because of your emotions.

- Don't be discouraged if you are slow to pick up all job responsibilities.

- Don't give up or avoid tasks due to your emotions.

- Don't be afraid to try new things.

- Don't hesitate to say, "I don't know."

- Don't hesitate to ask for more training or help.

SCRIPT

You: *I am really nervous to start my new job at Subline.*

Friend: *Slick Vic, you will do great! You just need to work hard and stay positive. You are going to start making some money to save up for a new TV.*

You: *Thanks, but what if I don't understand the job fast enough?*

Friend: *It happens to a lot of people. Make sure you make a friend at work and ask them questions. Most people will help you if you ask.*

You: *Thanks, bud!*

DISCUSSION QUESTIONS

1. What are some self-calming strategies you can do before starting a new job?
2. What are some things you should avoid to make sure your first day goes well?
3. How do you know when to ask questions of your co-workers?
4. What should you do if you really do not enjoy your new job?
5. What should you do if you do not fit in right away?

SELF-ASSESSMENT

Directions: Answer the question and give yourself a score of 1, 2, or 3 based on the description below. Take the quiz multiple times during the next few months to see if you are improving.

Do I manage my emotions well when starting a new job?

1 = I struggle with this issue and it causes problems.
2 = I still need some help but issues rarely happen.
3 = I understand this issue and do it well.

DO I USE THE INTERNET RESPONSIBLY AT WORK?

DO

DON'T

- Do only use the Internet for work-related tasks.

- Do recognize that co-workers might not be using the Internet appropriately, but that does not mean you should do the same.

- Do email co-workers about work-related topics.

- Do respond to emails within forty-eight hours or less (unless it's during a holiday).

- Do understand that you can be fired for breaking the Internet policy (specifically for using X-rated materials). If you are unsure about the boundaries, ask.

- Do consider how your social media posts outside of work could be viewed as offensive or hurtful.

- Do ask questions if you are unsure how to use work-related programs.

- Don't initiate small talk via email without a work-related purpose.

- Don't check personal accounts during work time.

- Don't go to non-work-related websites.

- Don't post on social media while you are at work.

- Don't use company Wi-Fi for your personal devices.

- Don't play games on the Internet or computer at work.

- Don't complain about work on social media.

SCRIPT

Co-worker: *I really want to know who is winning in the big basketball tournament!*

You: *I have them all recording on my DVR at home. Too bad we can't watch them here!*

Co-worker: *Yeah, me, too. I suppose I better get back to answering these emails.*

You: *Yeah, back to work!*

DISCUSSION QUESTIONS

1. What would you do if someone emails you about personal issues?
2. What is appropriate to do on your break?
3. What would you do if one of your co-workers said something offensive on social media?

SELF-ASSESSMENT

Directions: Answer the question and give yourself a score of 1, 2, or 3 based on the description below. Take the quiz multiple times during the next few months to see if you are improving.

Do I use the Internet responsibly at work?

1 = I struggle with this issue and it causes problems.

2 = I still need some help but issues rarely happen.

3 = I understand this issue and do it well.

COMMUNITY

DO I KNOW HOW TO TALK TO PEOPLE IN THE COMMUNITY?

- Do be friendly and smile at people if you make eye contact.

- Do stop talking to them if they seem uninterested.

- Do comment on obvious things you have in common if they look friendly.

- Do say "excuse me" if you are accidentally in someone's space.

- Do talk about topics related to the situation or area you are in.

- Do avoid confrontation if possible.

- Don't get in people's personal space.

- Don't talk to everyone.

- Don't talk to young kids if you are alone.

- Don't talk to people who look unsafe or unapproachable.

- Don't bring up any controversial topics.

- Don't assume every person wants to talk to you.

SCRIPT

You (while standing in line for concessions): *Hey, have you seen this band before?*

Stranger in the community: *No, this is my first time.*

You: *Awesome. They are really good.*

Stranger: *Yeah, I am having a great time.*

DISCUSSION QUESTIONS

1. What are examples of places where you could relate to people and have conversations with them?
2. When and how should you end a conversation with someone you just met?
3. What are some ways that you could make it awkward?
4. What are some ways that you could become friends?

SELF-ASSESSMENT

Directions: Answer the question and give yourself a score of 1, 2, or 3 based on the description below. Take the quiz multiple times during the next few months to see if you are improving.

Do I know how to talk to people in the community?

1 = I struggle with this issue and it causes problems.

2 = I still need some help but issues rarely happen.

3 = I understand this issue and do it well.

DO I KNOW HOW TO GET HELP IN PUBLIC?

DO

DON'T

- Do seek out community helpers such as police officers, firefighters, and mailmen.

- Do evaluate if someone looks safe before approaching him or her.

- Do call 911 if it is an emergency situation.

- Do be clear about what you need.

- Do make eye contact with the person you are talking to.

- Do leave the person alone if he or she seems busy.

- Don't make small talk.

- Don't interrupt people who are having a conversation unless it's an emergency.

- Don't approach people you view as unsafe, even if it's just a feeling that you have.

- Don't startle someone when trying to get his or her attention.

- Don't make the conversation any longer than it needs to be.

- Don't let someone take advantage of you because he or she helped you (such as asking for money, favors, or tips).

SCRIPT

You: *Hey, do you know where Dani's Taco Truck is?*

Stranger: *Yes, that place is so good! It's on the corner of Shad Lane and Gertrude Court.*

You: *Thanks so much.*

DISCUSSION QUESTIONS

1. How can you tell if someone is a safe or an unsafe person to talk to?
2. What should you do if you feel the person is unsafe after you begin the conversation?
3. When should you figure it out on your own versus when to ask for help?
4. What kinds of things should you not ask for help with?

SELF-ASSESSMENT

Directions: Answer the question and give yourself a score of 1, 2, or 3 based on the description below. Take the quiz multiple times during the next few months to see if you are improving.

Do I know how to get help in public?

1 = I struggle with this issue and it causes problems.

2 = I still need some help but issues rarely happen.

3 = I understand this issue and do it well.

DO I KNOW HOW TO INTERACT WITH POLICE?

- Do be polite.

- Do be cooperative and respond to small talk conversation with the police.

- Do use police as a resource.

- Do realize that police are just trying to keep the community safe.

- Do ask for a lawyer if needed.

- Do know your rights.

- Don't swear at the police.

- Don't refuse to follow police directions.

- Don't display a negative attitude toward the police.

- Don't call police for something that you can handle on your own.

- Don't be afraid of the police.

- Don't run from the police.

- Don't touch police officers except in friendly interactions (high fives, fist bumps, and hand shakes).

SCRIPT

You: *Good morning, officer. Do you know where the closest gas station is? I am running out of gas.*

Police Officer: *Yep, it's just up the road. Would you like me to follow you to make sure you make it?*

You: *Yes, that would be great. Thank you very much, Officer Eric.*

DISCUSSION QUESTIONS

1. What are some examples of things that you shouldn't say to the police?

2. What are some ways that police can help you?

3. What are some examples of when you should and should not call the police?

SELF-ASSESSMENT

Directions: Answer the question and give yourself a score of 1, 2, or 3 based on the description below. Take the quiz multiple times during the next few months to see if you are improving.

Do I know how to interact with police?

1 = I struggle with this issue and it causes problems.

2 = I still need some help but issues rarely happen.

3 = I understand this issue and do it well.

DO I FOLLOW SOCIAL RULES WHEN USING PUBLIC BATHROOMS?

DO

- Do give people more personal space than normal when in the bathroom.

- Do wash your hands each time you go to the bathroom.

- Do check your hygiene.

- Do try to leave at least one urinal between you and the next person if possible.

- Do use the stall if there is only one urinal free and two people are in the bathroom.

- Do try to keep your personal body parts covered as much as possible.

- Do clean up after yourself.

DON'T

- Don't look at other people while in the bathroom.

- Don't start up conversations in the bathroom.

- Don't make sounds while in the bathroom.

- Don't look through the stall doors.

- Don't talk on the phone in the bathroom.

- Don't touch anyone.

- Don't take more clothes off than you absolutely have to.

- Don't throw personal hygiene products in the toilet.

SCRIPT

You: (No script. Avoid eye contact. Go to the bathroom, wash your hands, and leave.)

DISCUSSION QUESTIONS

1. What should you do if someone talks to you in the bathroom?
2. How would you cover up sounds that you don't want others to hear in the bathroom?
3. Why do females tend to go in groups to the bathroom, while men tend to go alone?
4. How do you feel about people who don't wash their hands?

SELF–ASSESSMENT

Directions: Answer the question and give yourself a score of 1, 2, or 3 based on the description below. Take the quiz multiple times during the next few months to see if you are improving.

Do I follow social rules when using public bathrooms?

1 = I struggle with this issue and it causes problems.

2 = I still need some help but issues rarely happen.

3 = I understand this issue and do it well.

DO I FOLLOW SOCIAL RULES WHEN USING LOCKER ROOMS?

DO

DON'T

- Do keep your private areas covered as much as possible.

- Do pick a locker that is not close to other people's lockers.

- Do make sure to put all of your items in a locker.

- Do take up as little space as possible if the room is crowded.

- Do lock up any valuables.

- Do only use one locker.

- Don't make eye contact with others while changing.

- Don't initiate conversation when private areas are not covered.

- Don't talk too loudly.

- Don't use your phone in the locker room.

- Don't leave your clothes or items everywhere.

- Don't look or point at people.

- Don't go through other people's stuff.

SCRIPT

You: *Hey, tomorrow is arms day. I'll be there at four thirty.*

Friend: *Great, I will see you then.*

(Keep conversations brief in the locker room.)

DISCUSSION QUESTIONS

1. What can you do if the locker room is really crowded?

2. What would you do if someone you don't know starts talking to you?

3. What should you do if someone is looking at you while you are changing?

SELF-ASSESSMENT

Directions: Answer the question and give yourself a score of 1, 2, or 3 based on the description below. Take the quiz multiple times during the next few months to see if you are improving.

Do I follow social rules when using locker rooms?

1 = I struggle with this issue and it causes problems.

2 = I still need some help but issues rarely happen.

3 = I understand this issue and do it well.

DO I UNDERSTAND SOCIAL RULES
AT THE GYM?

DO

DON'T

- Do clean up after yourself.

- Do wipe down equipment when you are finished with it.

- Do greet people and smile if you make eye contact with someone.

- Do realize that the gym can be a place to make friends, but not everyone is looking to make friends.

- Do give more personal space to people in the gym than you typically would.

- Do wear appropriate gym attire. (See Socially Appropriate Attire Examples in the Resource section of this book.)

- Don't initiate conversation with someone who is wearing headphones.

- Don't claim two machines at once if the gym is busy.

- Don't take another person's machine if he or she takes a break.

- Don't stare at people.

- Don't make lots of noises when you work out.

- Don't lift or do more than you can handle.

- Don't try to show off.

SCRIPT

You: *Hey, could you spot me?*

Random gym person: *Sure. How many reps are you trying to get?*

You: *Thanks. I am trying to get ten.*

DISCUSSION QUESTIONS

1. What should you do if someone takes your machine?
2. What should you do if someone talks to you too much?
3. How can you make friends/relationships at the gym?

SELF-ASSESSMENT

Directions: Answer the question and give yourself a score of 1, 2, or 3 based on the description below. Take the quiz multiple times during the next few months to see if you are improving.

Do I understand social rules at the gym?

1 = I struggle with this issue and it causes problems.

2 = I still need some help but issues rarely happen.

3 = I understand this issue and do it well.

DO I KNOW HOW TO USE THE SIDEWALK?

DO

DON'T

- Do keep to the right side of the sidewalk.

- Do be aware of others who might be faster or slower than you.

- Do greet others with a smile or "hi" in passing.

- Do be aware of surroundings and potentially dangerous people/ situations.

- Do warn others if you are coming up behind them.

- Do clean up your pet's messes.

- Don't take up too much space by walking in the middle of the sidewalk.

- Don't sit on the trail.

- Don't litter.

- Don't have full conversations with unfamiliar people because they are most likely busy.

- Don't make continuous eye contact

SCRIPT

You: (While passing someone) *Good morning.*

Stranger in passing: *Hey there. Great morning for a walk.*

You: *Sure is.* (Smile and continue on walk, run, etc.)

DISCUSSION QUESTIONS

1. What should you do if someone is in your way?
2. What should you do if you feel unsafe?
3. What should you do if someone tries to have a full conversation with you?
4. What should you do if someone joins you while walking or running?

SELF-ASSESSMENT

Directions: Answer the question and give yourself a score of 1, 2, or 3 based on the description below. Take the quiz multiple times during the next few months to see if you are improving.

Do I know how to use the sidewalk?

1 = I struggle with this issue and it causes problems.

2 = I still need some help but issues rarely happen.

3 = I understand this issue and do it well.

DO I KNOW HOW TO INTERACT
WITH MY HIRED DRIVER?

DO

DON'T

- Do make some small talk.

- Do speak clearly and at a volume that the driver can hear.

- Do use "please" and "thank you."

- Do tell the driver if GPS is not accurate or if there is a "short cut."

- Do check for any items left in the car when you are leaving it.

- Do wear your seatbelt.

- Do tip the driver.

- Don't touch the driver.

- Don't share too many personal details.

- Don't leave items in the car.

- Don't fall asleep in the car.

- Don't make a mess in the car.

- Don't ask personal questions abou the driver.

- Don't argue or fight in the car.

- Don't distract the driver with your actions.

SCRIPT

Driver: *Good evening. Where are you headed tonight?*

You: *We are going to Stacie's Grill.*

Driver: *Perfect! It should only take us about ten minutes to get there. Have you ever had Stacie's chicken?*

You: *No. This is our first time going, but we heard from our friends that the place is awesome!*

Driver: (Ten minutes later.) *Okay, we are here. That will be seven dollars and fifty-nine cents.*

You: *Here's ten bucks. Thank you.*

DISCUSSION QUESTIONS

1. What should you do if the driver is rude?

2. What should you do if you share a cab?

3. What should you do if you feel unsafe in the cab?

4. What should you do if you cannot understand the driver?

SELF-ASSESSMENT

Directions: Answer the question and give yourself a score of 1, 2, or 3 based on the description below. Take the quiz multiple times during the next few months to see if you are improving.

Do I know how to interact with my hired driver?

1 = I struggle with this issue and it causes problems.

2 = I still need some help but issues rarely happen.

3 = I understand this issue and do it well.

DO I RIDE THE BUS WITHOUT ANY PROBLEMS?

DO

DON'T

- Do keep to yourself or talk to familiar people.

- Do greet the bus driver.

- Do use electronics if you wish.

- Do be aware of surroundings and potentially dangerous people or situations.

- Do keep track of your possessions.

- Do only bring what you can carry in one load.

- Do make small talk if people talk to you.

- Do realize when your stop is coming up.

- Don't take up too much space.

- Don't be too loud.

- Don't play your music too loudly.

- Don't kick the seat ahead of you.

- Don't sit next to someone if there are many open seats.

- Don't make a lot of small talk with people.

- Don't talk on your phone.

- Don't swear.

- Don't start arguments or fights.

SCRIPT

You: *Good morning.*

Bus Driver: *Mornin'. One dollar, please.*

You: (Pay one dollar and then sit in a seat.)

DISCUSSION QUESTIONS

1. What should you do if people near you are loud?
2. What should you do if you feel unsafe?
3. What should you do if someone will not stop talking to you?
4. What should you do if the bus is crowded?

SELF–ASSESSMENT

Directions: Answer the question and give yourself a score of 1, 2, or 3 based on the description below. Take the quiz multiple times during the next few months to see if you are improving.

Do I ride the bus without any problems?

1 = I struggle with this issue and it causes problems.

2 = I still need some help but issues rarely happen.

3 = I understand this issue and do it well.

DO I BEHAVE RESPECTFULLY AT THE MOVIES?

- Do turn your phone off.

- Do laugh at funny parts.

- Do stay in your seat unless you have to use the bathroom.

- Do use the bathroom before the show starts.

- Do stay quiet during the movie.

- Don't check your phone during the movie.

- Don't talk during the movie.

- Don't take your shoes off.

- Don't kick the seat ahead of you.

- Don't be too affectionate with another person while at the movies.

- Don't ask questions during the movie.

- Don't predict what is going to happen next.

SCRIPT

Friend: (Laughs at funny part.)
You: (No script. Be quiet during the movie.)

DISCUSSION QUESTIONS

1. What should you do if people near you are loud?
2. What could you do if you hate the movie and want to leave but your friends don't agree with you?
3. What should you do if you need to go to the bathroom during the middle of the movie?

SELF-ASSESSMENT

Directions: Answer the question and give yourself a score of 1, 2, or 3 based on the description below. Take the quiz multiple times during the next few months to see if you are improving.

Do I behave respectfully at the movies?

1 = I struggle with this issue and it causes problems.
2 = I still need some help but issues rarely happen.
3 = I understand this issue and do it well.

DO I INTERACT WELL WITH RESTAURANT STAFF?

- Do use "please" and "thank you" every time you ask for or receive something.

- Do make eye contact when talking or listening.

- Do answer all of the server's questions.

- Do tip at least 15 percent if it's a sit-down restaurant.

- Do talk clearly in a voice that can be heard by the server.

- Do put side conversations on hold when the server comes to the table.

- Do understand that mistakes happen and that the server has to serve more than just your table.

- Do wave and make eye contact if you need the server to come over.

- Do engage in some small talk.

- Don't make unnecessary requests.

- Don't be rude if your order is wrong.

- Don't ask for your meal to be fixed if you can fix it yourself.

- Don't leave notes or objects in place of tips.

- Don't purposely make a mess for the server to clean up.

- Don't mumble or talk so quietly that the server cannot understand you.

- Don't swear at the staff.

- Don't yell across the room or make a scene to get your server to come to your table.

- Don't talk too much to the server because it keeps them away from serving other tables.

SCRIPT

Friend: *Hey, did you guys get a chance to see wrestling last night? Chuck Towers took championship!*

You: *Yes, I did … (Server comes to the table.)*

Server: *How is your meal? Can I get you anything else?*

Friend: *Great. Could we have more napkins, please?*

Server: *Sure, I will bring those right over. (Server walks away.)*

You: *Yeah, I saw Chuck win it all. He is so hardcore.*

DISCUSSION QUESTIONS

1. What should you do if your order is incorrect?
2. How should you handle a rude server?
3. What would you do if you could not find your server or if they came too often to your table?
4. What would you do if you and your friends' bills are all on one check?
5. What are some ways to figure out how much to tip?

SELF-ASSESSMENT

Directions: Answer the question and give yourself a score of 1, 2, or 3 based on the description below. Take the quiz multiple times during the next few months to see if you are improving.

Do I interact well with restaurant staff?

1 = I struggle with this issue and it causes problems.

2 = I still need some help but issues rarely happen.

3 = I understand this issue and do it well.

DO I KNOW HOW TO CALL A STORE?

- Do start with small talk and ask how the person is doing.

- Do ask for the appropriate department.

- Do use "please" and "thank you."

- Do use a calm tone of voice.

- Do talk clearly at an even pace and take breaths in-between sentences.

- Do make a closing statement such as, "Thank you, have a nice day."

- Don't mumble or talk quietly.

- Don't talk too fast or too slow.

- Don't swear or show anger or frustration.

- Don't skip small talk.

- Don't keep the conversation long.

- Don't hang up without a closing statement.

- Don't hang up if put on hold.

SCRIPT

Store: *Hello, this is Joe from Game Palace. How can I help you?*

You: *Hello, do you have the new G-Cube?*

Store: *Hold on while I go look.*

You: (Wait.)

Store: *We currently have one. Would you like me to hold it for you?*

You: *Yes, thank you. You can hold it under [insert name].*

Store: *No problem. Anything else I can help you with?*

You: *No thank you. Have a good day.*

DISCUSSION QUESTIONS

1. What should you do if the employee is angry?
2. What would you do if the item was not in stock?
3. What would you do if you were on hold for too long?
4. What should you do if you get disconnected?

SELF-ASSESSMENT

Directions: Answer the question and give yourself a score of 1, 2, or 3 based on the description below. Take the quiz multiple times during the next few months to see if you are improving.

Do I know how to call a store?

1 = I struggle with this issue and it causes problems.

2 = I still need some help but issues rarely happen.

3 = I understand this issue and do it well.

RESOURCES

TONE OF VOICE

Tone of voice is important because it can change the meaning of what you are saying. The words are a very small percentage of the message you are sending. Your body language and tone of voice communicate how you feel about what you are saying. By practicing these exercises, you can improve your communication skills, which will help to sustain better relationships.

Tone of voice includes:

- Volume of your voice

- Pace at which you talk

- Pitch of your voice

TONE VARIATION EXERCISES

In the chart on the opposite page, read each sentence in each emotional tone (excited, bored, etc.). Using the scale below, rate yourself or have a partner rate you by putting a 1, 2, or 3 in each box.

1 = Wrong tone of voice for the situation

- People will understand what you are saying but could misinterpret how you feel about the situation.

2 = Flat tone / no tone variation

- People will understand what you are saying.

3 = Correct tone of voice for the situation

- People will both understand what you are saying and how you feel about the situation.

	Excited	Bored	Calm/ Relaxed	Sad	Sarcastic/ Joking	Frustrated	Serious
"Could you help me?"							
"Good morning."							
"I don't like that."							
"You are such a good friend."							
"I really like the present you gave me."							
"Sure, I'll get that done right away."							
"Thanks for your help."							
"Good to see you."							
"Sure, I'd like to hang out."							
"You have to be kidding me."							
"What's for lunch?"							
"I had such a good time."							
"Those are the rules."							

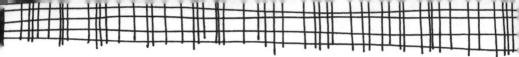

FACIAL EXPRESSION EXAMPLES

Your facial expression can communicate how you are feeling about a subject. Therefore, it is very important that the expressions you use are appropriate for the context. The wrong facial expression can hurt relationships and communicate messages that you are not feeling.

Happy / Content   Bored

Annoyed

Frustrated

Focused

Joking / Sarcastic

Nervous / Unsure

Sad / Hurting / Depressed

Confused

BODY LANGUAGE EXAMPLES

Body language is just as important as tone of voice and facial expression. People will assume how you feel on a subject based on the cues you send with your posture and face. Your body language will either help you or hurt you socially. Being able to read other people's body language will help you succeed socially and avoid offending people.

Flirty / Interested

Uninterested

Confident

Lazy

Nervous

Defensive

Relaxed / Calm

Impatient

Thinking / Evaluating

Disbelief / Doubt

Listening / Interested   Arrogant / Show off

SOCIALLY APPROPRIATE ATTIRE EXAMPLES

People judge how you dress. It is important to dress appropriately for the setting, and different settings call for different attire. If you dress against the social norm, people may exclude you. Dressing appropriately for the setting will help you make friends and fit in. Dressing for the setting will also help you at work.

People should be showered and clothes should be clean in all of the following scenarios.

Work

Gym

Date

Wedding

Home

Casual

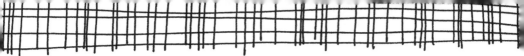

SELF–ASSESSMENT

This section is intended to allow you to view your progress in one snapshot. After reviewing each topic's dos and don'ts, mark 1, 2, or 3 based on your self-assessment on the topic. Re-score yourself in a new square every four to six weeks to assess your progress.

1 = I struggle with this issue and it causes problems.

2 = I still need some help but issues rarely happen.

3 = I understand this issue and do it well.

FAMILY

Do people feel like I am a good listener?						
Do I know how to accept gifts?						
Do I know how to admit I am wrong and say sorry?						
Do I know how to respond to someone talking about something I don't like?						
Do I know how and when to say no to family?						
Do I know how to act and talk when I am around family?						
Do I know what to do when other people fight or argue?						
Do I know how to plan a family event?						

NON—FAMILY RELATIONSHIPS

Do people think my house looks acceptable?						
Do I get along with my roommate?						
Do people think I am a good host?						
Do people think I am a good guest?						
Do I look presentable?						
Do I interact well in groups?						
Do I realize when my friends are bored?						
Do I know how to get out of uncomfortable situations?						
Do I know when I brag or talk about myself too much?						
Do I give people enough space?						
Do I know how to deal with secrets?						
Do I know how to respond to a friend who is sad?						
Do I know how and when to say no?						
Do I know how and when to text a friend?						
Do I know how to talk to a friend on the phone?						
Do I know how to use social media appropriately?						
Do I interact well with friends at restaurants?						
Do I know how to get a boyfriend or a girlfriend?						
Do I know how to maintain a relationship?						

WORK

Do people at work respect me?					
Do I chat well with my co-workers?					
Do I speak with my boss well?					
Do I know when people need space at work?					
Do I resolve my own conflict at work?					
Do I understand sarcasm at work?					
Do I manage my emotions well when starting a new job?					
Do I use the Internet responsibly at work?					

COMMUNITY

Do I know how to talk to people in the community?					
Do I know how to get help in public?					
Do I know how to interact with police?					
Do I follow social rules when using public bathrooms?					
Do I follow social rules when using locker rooms?					
Do I understand social rules at the gym?					
Do I know how to use the sidewalk?					
Do I know how to interact with my hired driver?					
Do I ride the bus without any problems?					
Do I behave respectfully at the movies?					
Do I interact well with restaurant staff?					
Do I know how to call a store?					

AUTHOR

Carlos Torres is an author, coach, and therapist. He creates curriculum and designs groups to develop social skills, vocational skills, leisure skills, and relationship skills. Additionally, he coaches special needs sports teams. Carlos' degree is in special education and he works full time helping at-risk children and young adults gain skills needed for independence.

AUTHOR

Katie Saint is a board-certified behavior analyst and licensed professional therapist. Katie presents locally and internationally on topics related to autism, mental health, and behavior analysis. Katie has a mental health counseling private practice and also is the director of training at an autism treatment program. Katie has designed college courses as well as published books and articles related to mental health.

ILLUSTRATOR

Michelle Lund is an artist and maker who creates in various mediums including pencil, fiber, silk-screen, clay, wood, textiles, and paint. She is a published illustrator and owns a kids and home creative business. Michelle loves living a homegrown, handmade life with her family on their homestead in rural Minnesota.